MOONTANGLED

A HARWOOD SPELLBOOK NOVELLA

STEPHANIE BURGIS

FIVE FATHOMS PRESS

This novella is dedicated to every single reader who asked me for a story about Miss Banks and Miss Fennell. I appreciate all of you so much!

MOONTANGLED

*D*ressing for a ball would always be a challenge for any lady who found it easier to analyze—from memory—an obscure spell from two centuries ago than to remember which sleeve lengths were currently fashionable across the nation. But dressing for a ball at Angland's first women's college of magic, where at least half the dancers were certain to add competitive spellwork to their costumes *and* the enigmatic local fey were likely to make an appearance? *That* raised the standards—and the stakes —enormously.

And when it came to selecting exactly the right outfit to entice one's own recalcitrant secret fiancée...

Well, it was lucky that Juliana Banks was used to tackling tricky challenges. It was even luckier that, for the first time in her life, she'd found a whole cohort of fellow women who understood her.

"*Definitely* not this gown *ever*," Ariana Stewart declared, her head buried in Juliana's wardrobe.

Hard on the heels of Ariana's words, Sujana Rao threw open the bedroom door without a knock and bustled inside, her slim figure nearly hidden behind the massive stack of clothes that filled her arms. "I *knew* she'd forget!" Sujana dropped her pile onto Juliana's bed with a *tsk*. "Don't bother looking through that pit of horrors, Ariana. I've been making notes for weeks about what to offer her tonight when she finally started to panic."

"I'm not quite *that* predictable," Juliana began...

...Just as the door opened once more and Anne Hammersley poked her auburn head inside. "Oh, good! I thought I'd find everyone here. Juliana forgot about the ball, didn't she? I knew she would."

"Ugh!" Juliana collapsed onto the bed with a groan, barely avoiding one of her own gowns that Ariana had tossed aside in disgust. "I did *not* forget," she said, "I only..."

The door opened even further as Willa Koh swept past Anne, a selection of masks dangling from her fingers. "She forgot it was *tonight,* didn't she?" said Willa. "Don't worry! I've got plenty of masks to spare. If we all put our heads together, we'll manage to fit her out nicely in time."

It *was* fortunate, Juliana reminded herself, that her classmates knew her well. It was only ever so slightly humiliating that they understood her *so* well.

"I might have remembered," she mumbled, "if it hadn't been for—"

"That end-of-term project that's not due for *two more months*?" Ariana inquired, still digging for unlikely treasure in the depths of the wardrobe, beneath Juliana's excess books and papers.

"You mean the one she finished two weeks ago but isn't *quite* certain is perfect yet?" Sujana rolled her eyes and pulled a sparkling blue and purple shawl from her pile to hold against Juliana.

"Oh, no." Anne's lips curved into a subtle smile as she closed the door and walked soft-footed across the room. Even after all these months, she still carried herself with the hesitation of a scholarship girl uncertain of her welcome among her classmates—but rueful knowledge filled her voice. "I'll wager she's already been asking our professors about the projects due at the *end* of the year."

"I don't believe it's any of those," said Willa firmly. "*I* think she's doing extra work, separate from our coursework, just for fun. And she's not even asking for extra credit!" She pointed at Juliana's guilty expression. "You see? I *told* you so!"

As her friends burst into gales of laughter, Juliana groaned and covered her eyes with her hands. "It's not like that!" she protested. "It's just—we have only four years to study with some of the cleverest magicians in the nation. So, if I just *happened* to ask Mr. Wrexham to recommend some added reading...and then those books *happened* to be particularly interesting, so I went looking in the library for more on the same subject...and then *those* threw up some particularly complicated equations that I had to work out, which distracted me so I thought we had another week to prepare—"

"*Mm-hmm.*" That response came from all four of her classmates at once, and their exaggeratedly weary tone was so outrageous that there really was only one possible reaction...at least for a lady who'd spent all of her life sneak-reading stolen magical texts.

At the ripe old age of three and twenty, she had finally found a home where she could use all of that formerly forbidden knowledge. So every piece of clothing from the bed and the floor shot up and then scattered, raining down in a heavy, fluttering shower of sparkle and color across four of the women Juliana loved most in the entire world.

"*Ahhh!*"

Screaming and laughing, they beat back the attacking garments with their bare hands...and then the magical battle began in earnest.

Spells shot across the room, sparkling and fizzing. Fireworks made of light showered overhead, letting off deafening cracks of thunder. Different gowns squared off against each other in mid-air as different women wrested magical control of each. Shawls wrapped themselves tightly around gowns and were beaten away with mask-ribbons.

It was an all-out, five-person magical duel of light and noise and the kind of joyous, childish silliness that Juliana had never once experienced before she'd arrived here as a full adult, finally safe and free and—

"*Ahem.*" The door slammed open.

Every piece of clothing fell to the floor as five young women froze in mutual, overwhelming panic.

Cassandra Harwood, the forbiddingly famous, undeniably powerful, and terrifyingly inspiring headmistress of Thornfell College of Magic, stood in the open doorway of Juliana's bedroom, one brown eyebrow raised as she surveyed the glittering destruction.

Juliana stared at the woman she'd heroworshipped for nearly all her life and felt her throat go dry. "I...ah, Miss Harwood, we were—I mean..."

Frantic glances flew across the room. Ariana said, "We...were preparing for the ball together?"

"So I see." Miss Harwood's lips twitched. "And so I *heard* from the rooms below, where we are currently entertaining the most prominent gentryfolk of the county, along with our carefully invited visitors from across the nation...and telling them all what *serious, trustworthy,* and *responsible* students we are training as England's first class of lady magicians."

"I'm so sorry!" Juliana winced. "We never meant—"

"Next time," said Miss Harwood firmly, "practice your *muffling* spells at the same time as your dueling skills, if you please." Shaking her head, she stepped backwards. "And do make certain your rooms are respectable by the time you leave for the ball tonight, or our poor housekeeper will tear her hair out, and we'll *all* be left with sticks for breakfast."

The door shut behind her. All five women slumped.

"Phew." Sujana threw herself back on the bed, spreading herself starfish-like across the scattered clothes. "I haven't had such an entertaining battle since the last time my cousins came to visit."

"You mean last weekend?" Willa patted her vivid scarlet gown and black chignon back into place. "I *thought* I heard a ruckus from your room while they were there."

Anne was already picking up the clothes from across the floor. "How long do we have left?"

"Well, if the guests are already here, then..." Ariana's voice chirped on, bright with interest, but Juliana couldn't take in a single word that followed.

The guests are here.

After all these months apart, Caroline was actually *here*. In this house. In the floor just below.

She's back. Memories cascaded over Juliana from the last visit, when the ruling Boudiccate had assigned Caroline Fennell, the assistant to one of their own most famous members, to their inspection team for Thornfell College of Magic.

Her eyes fell half-closed, remembering.

Warm breath brushing softly against Juliana's throat, tingling against the sensitive skin behind her ear as sensations overwhelmed her from every angle...

Warm hands sliding possessively up her sides,

unbuttoning the bodice of her gown with eager fingers. *"Finally..."*

And then that glassy-eyed, utterly distant look just one night later, when Juliana had slipped into Caroline's bedroom after everyone else had finally fallen asleep. She'd been so desperate to seize their last possible moment together before Caroline was sent off on her next political assignment...

But the woman who'd been her secret fiancée for years had looked up with a frozen, unnatural expression from the bed, and she had slowly shaken her head. *"I don't think this is a wise idea. Do you?"*

A stab of pain pierced Juliana's fingers now, and she belatedly realized that she had been clenching them.

Inside, she'd been clenched with panic ever since that moment, months ago, when she'd backed away in shocked silence and allowed the door to fall closed between them without even knowing why.

She was only tired and upset. Her aunt—her own mentor!—had been disgraced before all of us. She was grieving. She needed to be alone. That was all.

But that hadn't been the last stinging snub, had it?

No one could be allowed to know yet that they were betrothed, for the sake of Caroline's political career. Any ambitious lady politician, by national tradition, was expected to marry a magician before she could qualify for the dizzying heights of the Boudiccate—and until recently, the only acknowledged magicians in England had all been male.

Whenever their betrothal was officially

announced, the shock and controversy would polarize the nation. If they revealed it to the world too soon, before Juliana even held an official degree in magic, Caroline would be laughed off the political stage for good, her prospects dashed for years to come.

Juliana had always understood the necessity of discretion. It was why she had tried so hard to carefully ignore Caroline every time they'd met in public over the past year...just as Caroline had so *successfully* ignored her under everyone else's gaze.

But no one else could read the contents of their private letters. So why had Caroline's missives become so brief ever since her last visit to Thornfell?

Brief wasn't the word for those soulless mockeries. She'd written short letters before that Juliana still cherished for their passion. These, on the other hand...these letters were every bit as careless, entertaining, and impersonal as if she'd addressed a casual friend or political connection. Every single one had felt like a slap against Juliana's unshielded face with her fiancée's elegant, expensive riding gloves.

I will fix this, Juliana promised herself. *Tonight. I must.*

Despite what her new friends might think, scholarly interest wasn't the only reason she had buried herself so obsessively in her studies ever since the term began. The deeper she lost herself in her books, the less time she spent agonizing over what else she might be losing...and how she could ever put herself back together again afterwards.

"Juliana...*Juliana*!"

She jerked back to attention to find the other four shaking their heads at her.

"Thinking about those equations again," Sujana said dolefully. "If we weren't here—"

"It's a good thing we are," said Willa briskly. "But since we only have fifteen minutes left before we need to start our own preparations—"

"Wait." Juliana frowned. "That won't give you nearly enough time. Don't be silly!" She flapped her fingers at all of them in a shoo-ing gesture. "Don't waste any more of your evening here with me! I'm sure I can throw something together for myself from everything you've brought."

"Mmm..." Anne winced.

"You could," said Ariana, more diplomatically, "but we'd *prefer* to help you."

"You don't want to make a mess of it," said Willa. "Tonight's too important for that."

Oh no. Had Juliana slipped up during Caroline's last visit? "I...don't know what you mean?"

"Oh, no?" Sujana raised her eyebrows skeptically. "Come, now. I know you don't care for politics, but still —hasn't it even occurred to you? All those carefully invited visitors Miss Harwood mentioned: don't you think we ought to make a good impression on them, as England's first-ever class of female magicians? It would be nice to win ourselves a chance at being hired one day—*and* prove we aren't destined to ruin the nation forever, no matter what all those pundits in the newspapers might claim."

Juliana winced. "You really think I would dress *that* badly?"

"Don't be absurd." Ariana plopped herself comfortably onto the bed on Juliana's other side. "We're not afraid that you'll shame us. We're afraid that *you'll* lose a golden opportunity. This, tonight, is our best chance to impress some of the most influential people we'll ever meet. Don't you even want to try?"

"*You're* the whole reason this school was founded," Sujana said. "*You* were the one who went to Miss Harwood and begged her to teach you—which gave her the idea for Thornfell in the first place."

"I'd still be on my family's farm," said Anne softly, "dreaming of magic without a spellbook in sight if it weren't for you."

"And *you're* the reason I can finally study magic," said Willa, "without allowing people to keep on thinking I'm a man." Her nostrils flared with irritation. "Do you think any of us would allow you *not* to make the best possible impression on our visitors tonight?"

Juliana blinked rapidly as the three other women echoed Willa, their voices surrounding her in a chorus.

They were right. It *was* important that she make a good impression tonight...and not only for her magical career. But as she looked around, she realized something even more important.

No matter what happens tonight, I won't shatter after all.

...Even if the love of her life turned her away again.

...And even if it really wasn't possible to repair that precious, tingling connection that had carried her through the last three years, ever since she and Caroline had first met and she'd glimpsed a dazzling joy that she could never have imagined in her own family's bitter, disapproving household.

If she lost Caroline, it would break her heart. But she *would* survive and heal, because for the first time ever, she was surrounded by a sisterhood of women who valued her for who she truly was, flaws included.

"In that case, ladies..." Juliana gestured grandly at the gowns scattered all across the room, putting herself into her friends' hands without any more hesitation. "Get to work!"

Caroline Fennell might be one of the nation's fastest-rising political stars—but she could have no idea of what was about to hit her.

Juliana was here.

In this house.

Quite possibly—judging by those distracting thumps and shrieks of laughter that had sounded through the ceiling before Miss Harwood had sailed off to silence them—*directly* overhead.

Caroline's fingers tightened around her glass of elven wine as her breath shortened uncontrollably. She fought to keep her expression attentive to the conversation around her, no matter where her dangerous thoughts might stray. *Don't even think about going up there.*

She'd trained her willpower into a steel blade over the years—but the irrepressible images swam before her anyway, all the more vivid for the months she'd forced herself to stay away. Juliana would no doubt be preparing at the very last moment, as usual—quite possibly with a book still held in one hand. Her dreamy blue gaze would rest on the open page as she slowly, slowly slid her day gown off those slim white shoulders and then—

"What do *you* think of it all, Miss Fennell?"

Caroline crashed back into reality to find everyone in her conversational group awaiting her answer to the local justice of the peace's question.

Luckily, there was only one possible subject that anyone would discuss in lowered voices tonight while the headmistress of Thornfell was out of the room. "It is an astonishing achievement," she said firmly. "Angland will be all the richer for this school."

"Hmm," said the justice of the peace, an elegant woman in her mid-fifties with a conservative dark gown and a skeptical twist to her mouth. "But then, you were part of the inspection team that decided to allow it in the first place, weren't you? You and—of course..."

Her words trailed off, and Caroline's face tightened, all visions of bare shoulders and other enticements draining away.

"My aunt, Lady Cosgrave," she said crisply. "Yes. We were both pleased to confirm the safety and viability of this school."

"*Such* a pity that Lady Cosgrave had to step down from the Boudiccate so suddenly afterwards," said the woman who stood beside the justice of the peace—another local landholder, Caroline recalled. Her face was alight with malicious glee. "And so young, too! Long before anyone would ever have expected her retirement."

Caroline kept her smile steady. "We all appreciate her decades of service to the nation."

"Indeed," said the justice of the peace. "She was one of the most admired women in all of Angland."

...*Was* being the operative word.

The justice's neighbor was twenty years younger and far less practiced in her subtleties. She edged closer, dropping her voice to a thrilling whisper. "One does hear the most disturbing rumors flying around—"

"Only," said Caroline, "if one listens to wild and uninformed rumors—which of course you ladies never would." She took one last swig of her elven wine and deposited it swiftly on the side table nearby. "Now, if you'll excuse me..."

Sweet, tingling bubbles lingered on her tongue as she stepped away, but they couldn't scrub the bitterness from her throat as she heard the murmurs break out behind her. *Rank stupidity.* She should have remained visibly unmoved. Her aunt had trained her to ignore all such provocations.

It was an irony beyond compare that the woman who'd spent all of Caroline's life preparing her to join the Boudiccate was now the single largest obstacle to her ever doing so. But it would have been naïve beyond compare to imagine that Honoria Cosgrave—who had co-ruled the nation in a blaze of high fashion and steely political conservativism for years—could retire decades early from her post without inciting a wildfire of speculation. Here at this school, the only witnesses to her crime had kept their word and held her secrets safe in return for her voluntary resignation from the Boudiccate—but that had allowed even wilder theories to spread in their place.

Caroline, as Lady Cosgrave's niece, protégée, and expected successor to her seat on the Boudiccate—if only that seat had waited to open until the expected time!—was the one to whom everyone looked for answers now...but whom no one trusted anymore.

She was irretrievably tarred by the mystery of her aunt's disappearance—not only from politics but from public life, as well. Rather than making her own rounds through the ballrooms of the nation, head held high, to face down the gossips in their gatherings, Lady Cosgrave had chosen to ignore all of her own past maxims and retire to her country estate to lick her wounds in privacy...leaving Caroline to face all of the aftermath.

Damn you, Aunt Honoria. I could hate you for that.

The crime itself, Caroline had forgiven instantly. How could she not? Her aunt had acted to protect the woman she still loved, no matter how unorthodox and long-ended their romantic affair had been. Caroline would do the same in a heartbeat...which was why she had accepted the invitation to tonight's ball, despite how agonizing she knew its ending would be.

Unlike her aunt, Caroline refused to hide from the consequences of what had occurred. It was long past time to think of what *Juliana* needed most, not simply what she, Caroline, still wanted so desperately that she would have killed to protect it from any other threat. And as Juliana was far too kind-hearted and loyal to make that ruthless move on her own behalf...

It was time for Caroline to break their secret betrothal.

First, though, there was a ball to navigate, with more than one kind of dance to maneuver.

"Ladies and gentlemen!" Amy Harwood, the newest and most controversial member of the Boudic-cate, stood in the open doorway of the room, resplendent in crimson silk, with her golden torc of office gleaming around her dark brown neck and her good-natured—but shockingly unmagical—husband smiling behind her. As one of the highest politicians in the land and the official patroness of Thornfell College of Magic, Mrs. Harwood would have possessed a natural authority regardless—but this school stood on ancient Harwood land. Here, as the official head of the family, Amy Harwood had ruled supreme for years.

She was one of the politicians Caroline had always admired most, a leader who combined deep compassion with keen insight and a ruthless disdain for any traditions that held back the greater good of their nation. She had also been Aunt Honoria's closest friend for nearly all of Caroline's life.

That had ended nearly a year ago, when Honoria had first been blackmailed into dropping their connection. Worse yet, Aunt Honoria had chosen herself to betray that old friendship through her covert actions during the Boudiccate's inspection of this school, which had endangered Amy's own family and nearly wrecked the school's chances forever.

Caroline had known nothing of Honoria's personal schemes and would never have agreed to her methods, for a whole multitude of private reasons—but who would ever be trusting enough to believe that?

It took all of Caroline's strength now to keep her chin raised and her politely smiling gaze tilted in the right direction...until Amy Harwood's warm, intelligent gaze met hers on its sweep across the room.

Caroline's eyelids fell shut in instinctive, miserable self-defense.

She should have taken a second glass of elven wine after all.

Mrs. Harwood's voice filled the room like a bell, inescapable. "It's time to step into our gardens and discover the magical welcome our students have prepared for you."

A wave of intrigued murmurs swept through the

glittering crowd. As the good, the great, and the unrepentantly loathsome among the invited attendees all swarmed forward, Caroline opened her eyes and set her face into the practiced political smile that she'd learned to wear as a mask long ago. It was time to prove that she did have a conscience, no matter what anyone else in the nation thought.

She'd learned to make ruthless sacrifices seventeen years ago, when her political apprenticeship had first begun at the unusual age of eight. Now she was fiercely grateful for that early training—because without it, she could never have walked calmly forward to break her own heart.

* * *

GOLDEN LIGHTS GLIMMERED across the grass, lighting a sparkling path through the moonlight. Juliana, waiting with the others in the enspelled blackness of the garden beyond, held her breath as she watched Thornfell's great doors open wide. Light streamed out from the foyer, and guests streamed out with it in a chattering, glittering crowd.

Of course she'd never glimpse Caroline among so many others and from this distance—

There.

She'd know that haughty head-tilt anywhere—and oh, that easy, confident glide, like a panther prowling across the grass. There was only one thing missing: the usual laughing, vibrant circle of friends and admirers that followed Caroline Fennell to every social event of note.

Her breath escaped in a sigh of pure relief. It would be *so much* easier to tempt her fiancée discreetly into the shadows without any close observers keeping watch on them. Was that—*could* that be why Caroline had come alone to a party, for once? If she, too, was hoping for convenient privacy...

Warmth blossomed in Juliana's chest.

Behind her, Sujana whispered, "Ready...and...*now*!"

Magical fireworks showered above the grass beyond as the garden blazed into triumphant, golden life at the end of their path, a brightly-lit stage before the vast, dark woods that hulked beyond. An invisible symphony of strings, flutes, and drums filled the warm air, while victorious scenes from the nation's past stretched across the night sky, flashing from one famous triumph to another in dazzling succession.

The crowd came to a gasping, breathless halt, every head tipping back to take in each glittering, vivid detail...

Every head except for one.

Caroline's gaze fixed on Juliana across all the space between them—and *held*, as if no one and nothing else existed.

It was exactly the way she had looked at her that very first evening years ago, when the famous Miss Fennell had arrived as an invited guest to one of Juliana's aunt's crowded Winter Solstice house parties...and had looked straight through all the rising politicians and hopeful gentleman mages to where Juliana had stood in the shadows, hiding every passionate truth about herself for her own safety.

Caroline had *seen* her from the very beginning... and when Caroline looked at her like that, Juliana could almost believe that she really was as strong and as beautiful as Caroline claimed, no matter what her own aunt and father had always told her to the contrary.

She had vowed never to think about them again. She was free now, she was surrounded by friends, and Caroline still wanted her after all. The joy and relief of that was inexpressible.

She barely held herself back as the fireworks ended and Miss Harwood stepped into place between the visitors and the brightly-lit garden.

"Welcome to Thornfell College of Magic," said their headmistress. "You are all invited to walk the garden paths—and, of course, join the dance!"

The lighted path across the grass shot outward at her words, until it formed a massive, golden dance-floor. Glasses of elven wine floated in mid-air at the sidelines, waiting.

The music shifted into a jaunty new tune. Miss Harwood reached for her tall, lean husband to lead the dance. Juliana's fellow students surged forwards to join them—

And Juliana held Caroline's gaze as she shifted, deliberately, out from among all of her friends to slip into the shadows.

She didn't have to wait for long.

"Is it safe to steal a moment in private?" Caroline's words ghosted through the darkness, sending shivers down the back of Juliana's neck.

"This way," Juliana whispered, and led Caroline into the woods.

It was perfectly safe to enter at this time of year, so long as one stayed on the permitted paths. The fey and the Harwoods had struck a bargain centuries ago, one that had been renewed last year by the enigmatic protector of those woods. No fey would harm them if they kept the peace.

Still, the eeriness felt inescapable as they left the music and the lights behind them…and Caroline, inexplicably, stopped a good three feet away from her.

Casting a warm, inviting glow of light between them with a whispered spell, Juliana started forward.

Caroline held up a hand to stop her. "Wait." Her voice was flat; her expression impenetrable. "I have to tell you something."

Juliana froze. Half a dozen different responses flew to her lips and were discarded.

Naturally, only the most idiotic response broke through. "What do you think of my gown?"

Her eyes fell shut in utter chagrin.

This was part of why she'd never entered politics. But she'd never struggled to find the right words around Caroline before.

Caroline cleared her throat. "It looks…lovely. Truly lovely. And very fashionable."

"Ha." Juliana opened her eyes with a rueful sigh. "That's because I didn't pick it," she admitted. "The others—"

"Juliana." Caroline's voice wasn't loud, but her tone stopped Juliana immediately. "Listen. Please."

"I'm listening," Juliana whispered.

She had never listened so hard in her life, nor felt so much dread as she did.

"Things have changed in the past few months," said Caroline.

"What things?" The words came out as a strangled croak...and filled her with burning shame.

She'd never before been this slow to understand rejection.

You know exactly what's changed, Juliana's inner voice taunted. *It's how she feels about you.*

Those meaningless letters...that awkward final night last year...

She'd been so young when her family had taught her not to expect any affection to last. But she'd come here to fight for what she wanted—and she *did* still know that Caroline wanted her, didn't she?

Summoning all of her courage, Juliana stepped forward, reaching out to touch the bare skin of Caroline's strong fore-arm.

For the first time ever, Caroline shifted away from her touch, leaving Juliana's hand to fall away, unanchored. "I can't do this anymore. Not to you."

Pain wrenched a gasp from Juliana's chest. "Caroline—"

"No!" Caroline shook her head, her face contorting. "You don't understand because you've never cared for politics, but ever since Aunt Honoria resigned her seat, *everything* has changed. When we first met, I promised you something I can't give you anymore. I—"

"Something you can't give?" Juliana's voice spiraled against her will. "I'm not asking for anything different than I ever have before!"

"But I was supposed to be a sure thing." Caroline's words grated out like rusty steel as her eyes fell away from Juliana's face. Could she really not even bear to look at Juliana anymore? "*Everything* was safely planned. Everything was assured, from the time I was eight years old and my aunt first took me in as her apprentice! It was a certainty I'd take her place in the Boudiccate, despite any difficulties along the way. You and I could have faced down all the naysayers and risen together once you graduated. But now, with Aunt Honoria so publicly disgraced—"

"*Oh.*" Juliana almost staggered with the blow of it.

So *that* was why everything had changed last year! No wonder Caroline had looked so stunned and sick that final night...and no wonder Caroline had turned Juliana away after hearing her aunt's confession.

She had lost her sponsor. She had lost all of her surety.

How could Juliana not have seen it before?

Caroline could have afforded the political risk of their betrothal, back when everything about her future had been assured. But now, when she risked losing it all...

How could Juliana possibly be enough to make up for it?

"I understand," she whispered.

She had had years of practice, in her family home, at keeping all of her pain safely closed within herself. None of her skills or dreams had ever been enough for anyone there, either.

Had Caroline already decided on the most appropriate gentleman mage to wed now, to further her own career?

Had Juliana ever met him?

Her fingers tightened against the silk skirts of her gown.

"You understand? Really?" There was a lilt of surprise in Caroline's tone.

It was anything but flattering.

"You needn't worry." Juliana heard the bitterness leak like vinegar into her tone, but she couldn't hold it back. "I won't taint your reputation with a public scene."

"I didn't think you would." Caroline's frown was in her voice. "But Julie..."

"*Don't call me that!*" The words burst out against her will.

That was a private nickname. It was part of their love—secret and protected against the world.

She *never* wanted to hear it from Caroline's lips ever again.

"You should go back to the ball." She bit out the words, looking away from her ex-fiancée. "I'll come back later, so no one glimpses us together. That would be safest, wouldn't it?"

She heard Caroline's harshly indrawn breath...then her too-familiar voice, ringing with an irrational note of hurt. "If that's what you'd prefer."

Juliana couldn't find any response within herself to *that* absurdity. She only stood, in her pathetically borrowed gown and jewelry, hugging her aching chest in the darkness as the woman who'd promised to love her forever turned and walked away, heading toward the bright lights and the gaiety beyond...where she had always belonged, from the very beginning.

Juliana's family had been right about her after all. She and her awkward, inconvenient truths all belonged in the shadows...no matter what Caroline Fennell had tempted her to believe for a few shining years of possibility.

She had friends now, at least. She had a safe home to return to...and she *would*, as soon as it was possible again. But no one else could be allowed to glimpse the humiliation and heartbreak that had no place at Thornfell's triumphant ball tonight, before all of their watchful visitors.

For now, she only waited until Caroline was out of hearing range before she turned and fled, tears streaming down her cheeks, deep into the fey-ruled wood where no one else could find her.

* * *

IT WAS UNNERVING to walk without feeling one's own legs. They must still be moving, though, somehow—Caroline was halfway through the garden before she even came back into herself enough to understand exactly where she was, and that those moving blurs around her were fellow guests, chatting and swirling through the familiar dance of party protocol.

She knew that dance. She'd been following its steps since she was a still-homesick nine-year-old girl, sent away from her own family a year ago to make her fortune, obediently parroting key facts about everyone she met to her fabulously powerful and all-knowing aunt so they could discuss the best methods of influence.

One guest reached out to her now, leaking a trilling stream of words that were utterly incomprehensible.

The idea of summoning up any sort of response was absurd.

She kept moving past every attempted interruption, propelling herself forward somehow although everything beneath her chest seemed to have fallen away from her completely.

Perhaps it was only that the gaping wound in her chest was so insistent, no other pain could possibly compete with it.

There was a full glass of elven wine floating in the air ahead, unclaimed. She aimed for it with every ounce of the determination that had once powered her way up the ranks of local council, larger county, and even national infrastructures before she'd reached twenty years of age.

This goal was *far* more vital than any of those ever had been.

Her hand closed around the cool, damp stem of the glass with a visceral relief that nearly made her weep…

And a husky female voice whispered directly in her ear. "*Caroline.*"

The glass slipped from her fingers to fall upon the grass as she jerked around.

It wasn't Juliana, of course, who stood watching her from the shadows. It wasn't a human woman at all.

The woman who stood in the shadows just beyond the gleaming dance floor—her long, loose hair tangled with leaves and her eyes shining like a cat's with reflected candlelight—was one she had seen only once before, on a pitch-dark night in the middle of those neighboring, fey-ruled woods at the very height of the dangerous bluebell season. That night, Caroline had watched Aunt Honoria confess that she had arranged the abduction and disposal of another member of the ruling Boudiccate…with the forbidden help of a centuries-old fey guardian so powerful that her sinister, thorn-studded vines had stretched in through the protected windows of Thornfell itself, past every magical ward and barrier, to seize one of the most dangerous women in all of Angland from her bed.

Rajaram Wrexham himself, one of the Boudiccate's most brilliant officers of magic, had once been taken prisoner by those vines. Caroline carried no delusions that she could defend herself now.

A chill rippled through her body. She could only summon up a distant memory of pride to keep her voice from shaking as she replied. "I'm afraid you have the advantage of me, madam. We have not yet been introduced."

The woman's smile revealed sharp, glinting teeth. "Young ones," she murmured. "So impatient. I've only ever offered my true name to one human."

Of course—the Harwoods' most mysterious ancestor, a scholarly gentleman who'd secretly flouted the laws of his own era to swear his love to this powerful wild fey.

There'd been no happy ending to their love story, but rather a tragic misunderstanding that had led to over a century of misplaced bitterness—bitterness that had been played upon by Honoria last spring.

Caroline swallowed now, her throat suddenly terribly dry, as she accepted the fey rebuke. Clearly, there would be no refuge in pleasant small talk in this encounter...and there was only one reason why the Harwoods' most dangerous new ally would approach her and single her out by name.

"If you wish me to convey any message to my aunt, I—"

"Foolish girl." Branches poked out of the fey's loose brown hair as she shook her head, *tsk*'ing her long tongue against her sharp teeth. "Have you truly forgotten your own mistakes so quickly?"

27

"My…?" Caroline stared at her. Fizzy elven wine was soaking through her right slipper, but it felt too dangerous to move even an inch to avoid it. She swept her mind back through her last visit to Thornfell. She *hadn't* been included in any of her aunt's illicit plans—but did even Honoria's one accomplice not believe that? "Last year—"

"It's been scarcely ten minutes, now. I thought humans more attuned to passing time."

"Ten—?" *Oh!* Realization lurched through Caroline's gut. "What have you done to Juliana?" She lunged forward, kicking the discarded wine glass out of her way. "She's done no harm to anyone! Your own longstanding bargain with the Harwoods prevents—"

"Was *I* the one who hurt her this evening?"

Caroline's jaw dropped open in outrage as she took in the meaning behind those sly words. "I didn't hurt her! I was *protecting* her."

…And Juliana had only too readily agreed to that protection, hadn't she?

She had immediately *understood* the practical necessity of separating herself from Caroline's public shame.

She had agreed that their betrothal was no longer worthwhile.

She'd even pointedly sent Caroline away at the end to avoid being witnessed in the company of her politically-tarnished ex-fiancée before all those other important guests who had been summoned to the ball tonight.

Caroline had arrived at Thornfell determined to do the right thing...but she'd never even realized until this moment just how desperately she'd hoped for Juliana to refuse her noble sacrifice.

Worse yet, she hadn't understood how pathetically, unreasonably certain she had actually been that her fiancée was the one person in Angland who had truly cared for *her*, Caroline the woman, not the famously rising young politician Miss Fennell.

She should have learned better months ago, when the first of her old friends had so unceremoniously dropped her. It hadn't taken long for the others to follow suit, for eminently practical and understandable reasons.

Who would want to be associated with political poison?

"Our ancient agreement," whispered the guardian, "promises safety to any who remain on the set paths. There were no promises made for what would happen to anyone unwise enough to leave their protection."

Caroline frowned. "Juliana would never be so foolish." Her ex-fiancée had the sharpest brain for magic of anyone she'd ever met. After last year's crisis, Caroline was certain Juliana would have inhaled every book in the college library that related to local fey history. If even Caroline knew that basic magical rule, Juliana could certainly never forget it.

"No?" The fey raised her eyebrows, stepping backwards into the deeper shadows, until only her taunting voice floated out from within them. "Well, I suppose it was foolish to expect you to care for her danger, now that you've tossed her away. Human loves are so simple to discard, aren't they? Like autumn leaves, brushed aside before winter. You probably won't even miss her if she's trapped forever, will you?"

Caroline had spent all of her life studying diplomacy, debate, and clever strategic thinking. She had learned never to make a single move without formulating a careful plan beforehand.

Now she turned without a word of farewell, scooped up her skirts, and tore back to the woods as fast as her long legs would carry her, shoving past influential figures along the way and ignoring every outraged voice that called after her.

She'd lost every dream of her own that she'd cherished.

She wouldn't let Juliana be lost, too.

IT DIDN'T TAKE LONG for Juliana to stop running. Her borrowed gown—ever so slightly too long, despite the clever, hidden pins that held its skirts perfectly in place when she stood still or moved slowly—kept tangling awkwardly in her legs. Worse yet, she'd spent the entirety of the last year buried in books, without any of those long, laughing hikes in the open air that Caroline had once regularly swept her along.

She wouldn't think of those hikes now...but her faithless legs couldn't help remembering the difference. They were aching with unaccustomed exertion by the time she came to a stop, breathing hard.

The path that she had run along branched out in three different directions from this point, each one stretching deeper into the darkness of the woods. The broad base of a broken tree trunk sat in the middle of them all.

She clambered onto it and let her eyes fall closed as she sat back, bracing her hands on the damp and bumpy wood and tipping her head back to face the sky as her feet dangled several inches above the ground. Soft strands of moonlight trickled down through the thick canopy of leaves and branches, resting on her eyelids like a soothing touch from above.

So.

There was no more running to be done from the truth. Caroline had chosen political efficacy over love, just as Caroline's aunt had decades beforehand. *Of course* it hurt. It might never stop hurting. But Juliana had had a full year to prepare herself. Perhaps she might even find it within herself to be grateful one day for those brusque, brief letters that had paved the way to tonight's revelations. At least she hadn't been taken entirely off-guard by them.

It didn't feel noticeably better, though, to have her worst fear finally arrive.

There was a splinter poking sharply into her left palm. Sighing, she opened her eyes and lifted her hands to start the tedious work of digging it out, casting a minimal spell of light around the tiny, stinging dot.

She couldn't go back to Thornfell for hours, anyway. Too many of her friends were waiting in the brightly-lit grounds outside the woods, and they were all certain to notice that she had been weeping. Not to mention all of those sharp-eyed persons of influence whom they were meant to impress...

No. She shuddered. She could not make polite small talk with anyone tonight. She might be missed when it came time for the planned demonstrations of individual magic at the end of the evening, but it would be far better for Thornfell's reputation that she not attend in her current state. She would stay here instead until the evening was done, and only then, when everyone was safely gone...

"*Juliana.*"

The sudden, piercing whisper behind her made her jump. Scrambling awkwardly off her perch, she peered into the darkness of the thickly clustered trees.

"Who's there?"

Branches rustled, deep in the darkness. A sigh of wind ruffled through Juliana's hair and sent a prickling line of goosebumps down her neck.

A swirl of dancing silver lights flickered in the corner of her vision. She swung around.

Nothing. She stood alone, her own quick breaths loud in her ears.

She'd known she was venturing into fey territory, hadn't she?

They can't touch me if I stay on the path. That memory steadied her as she turned in a slow circle, careful where she placed her feet...and wondering, with a shivering intensity, just *how many* fey eyes were fixed on her in that lurking darkness.

But she knew the rules, didn't she? She was an excellent student. This was only one more exercise in the application of knowledge under pressure, like so many others she had completed over the last year of study. *So!*

"I am a student at Thornfell," she said clearly, "studying with Miss Cassandra Harwood. I apologize if I've intruded on your peace tonight."

High-pitched giggles burst out at her words, louder and louder and closer and closer, until they came from all around her, filling her ears, as if the woods itself was convulsing with malicious glee at her folly.

Juliana had never heard that predatory fey laughter before in her life, but her body recognized it all the way down to her bones. Terror of it had been bred into her ancestors on this misty, magic-drenched isle centuries ago. Now it took hold of her muscles and tried to send her fleeing for her life with no care for where she stumbled, just to escape from it.

Keep to the path. Keep to the path!

There was no safe direction for her to face that wouldn't leave her vulnerable from behind. She swallowed hard as she shifted, with flinching care, to place one foot squarely on the branch of the path that would lead her safely back to Thornfell. "I will leave you to your own entertainments tonight," she said, her voice shaking horribly. "But if you wish me to pass Miss Harwood any message when I return—"

"Miss Harwood, she says!"

"Miss Harwood? Doesn't she know?"

"Harwood's *not calling her."*

"She's not the one calling your name."

"*'Juliana! Juliana! Juliana!'"* The taunting voices circled round and round her on the path. *"Can't you hear her calling out to you now, deep in the tangles? Poor thing. Poor silly thing. 'Juliana!'"*

"'She?'" Juliana repeated in a whisper.

Her brain felt as if it had gone numb from fear. She knotted her fingers in her skirts, fighting to pierce the fog of confusion.

Had one of her friends come looking for her when they'd realized she was missing from the ball?

Keep to the path. Keep to the path. And never let them trick you!

Every student at Thornfell knew those rules. They would never be foolish enough to break them. If she hurried now, she might even catch up with them on the path ahead before they ventured too close to these mischief-makers. Then she could link arms with them and run all the way home.

All she had to do was keep her head for a few more minutes.

"Poor lost girl, still hunting for you."

"Poor Caroline..."

"Lost, lost, lost—"

"No!" Fury flooded through Juliana, dissipating the fog. "You cannot trick me that way. She left the woods! I watched her do it."

She left me, after all of her promises.

Like the elves, the fey never lied outright, but they could twist the truth into knots to waylay reckless travelers. She'd known that for years, from books and warnings. But for them to *dare* try to use her heartbreak against her, tonight of all nights—!

"She came back, though," a dozen voices caroled, giggling with malevolent delight. *"She came back. And this time, oh dear, she didn't stay on the path..."*

There was no way to misinterpret those words.

Certainty formed a cold, clear blade within her chest.

Hard-headed, strategic Caroline had never been so reckless before. But the fey never lied outright...

And Caroline *could not* be lost. Not ever, certainly not like this—and *especially* not before Juliana had had the chance to collar her faithless former fiancée and tell her *exactly* what she thought of all those broken promises!

She had done more than enough weeping and accepting tonight. What had she even been thinking earlier, to let Caroline go without a word of reproach? She was no longer that desperately lonely, tongue-tied girl who'd been taught by her family of birth that she was inherently unlovable, her magical talents useless to them and unwanted. She was an active magician in training now, and she'd found the home where she belonged. It was time to summon all of the magic she had learned and *fight.*

"Where. Is. She. Now?" She gritted the words through her teeth. "Lead me to her, and I'll strike a bargain with you."

"A bargain?"

"Ooh, a bargain!"

"How delicious!"

"But not with us."

"We're not the ones you'll have to bargain with to save her *life."*

"But we'll take you to her."

"Come this way, and you'll see."

"This way, Juliana...come this way..."

Sparks of silver danced invitingly in the dense trees to her left. They promised danger and temptation and, quite possibly, destruction.

But unlike her former fiancée, Juliana had *meant* all of her promises. So she lifted her chin, cast a ball of warm light firmly before her, and strode swiftly off the path in pursuit of the errant—and about to be *deeply* regretful—love of her life.

THE FURTHER CAROLINE forged into the woods, the more badly she wished that she had thought to bring a torch—or, better yet, that she had scooped up any of the many magicians who'd milled around the grounds of Thornfell, swilling elven wine and gossip. They'd do far more good here than she could on her own, stumbling around in the darkness without a plan—and she could only imagine the scathing commentary her aunt would have provided if she had witnessed Caroline's heedless race into the woods tonight, without a single moment of pause to formulate strategies or defenses.

Then again, if it weren't for Honoria's own thoughtless actions, Caroline wouldn't be here in the first place. She had been stumbling around in the dark, in one way or another, ever since that night last spring when all of her foundations had been yanked from beneath her feet.

Twigs cracked loudly beneath her feet and poked sharp points into her thin dancing slippers. A branch snagged her upswept hair and tugged so hard she nearly fell. With a wrench, Caroline forced herself to stop and stand still instead of lunging any further forward.

Taking a deep breath, she fisted her hands by her side and closed her eyes. *Think*. She laid out the situation in her head, the way Honoria had taught her so many years ago. *First the facts, then the dangers, and only then the solution.*

Fact: She was far off the path of safety, with no magic and no light. No Harwood bargain protected her here...and the fey, unlike her, could see in the dark.

The dangers: Immeasurable no matter what she did from now on.

Therefore: there was no point in even trying to stay quiet any longer.

"Juliana!" she shouted as she untangled herself from the wayward branch. "Juliana! Where are you?"

Was that a whisper of laughter through the trees? Or only the wind and her imagination?

The path lay far behind her. It wasn't worth finding again, anyway. Not without the woman she'd sworn to protect.

She'd give up everything else in a heartbeat for that.

"Juliana!"

Her voice was hoarse with shouting by the time she stumbled once again to a stop countless minutes later, leaning heavily against the closest thick tree trunk. Her chest ached as she panted for breath. Her long hair fell around her shoulders, yanked free of its polished politician's coiffure. Her arms stung with scrapes—and they were probably bleeding, too.

Even if there *had* been light to see in these woods, no one would have recognized the famous Miss Fennell now.

Silver lights sparkled faintly in the distance. She blinked hard, straightening away from the tree's support.

They didn't disappear. Instead, they bounced forward, closer and closer, followed by a larger ball of light that floated steadily in mid-air just behind them.

The fey had finally found her.

Ice chilled Caroline's spine. She drew her shoulders back.

Good. Maybe they knew where Juliana was. It was

time to remember all of her training and *be* the dazzling politician that she should have become.

"My lords and ladies!" she called out. "I'd like to offer you a bargain. If—"

"Don't you dare speak another word, Caroline Fennell!" The voice that hissed out behind that floating ball of light was utterly furious...and unmistakably familiar.

"Juliana?" Relief rushed through her body; Caroline grabbed hold of the rough tree trunk behind her for balance as her knees gave out beneath her. "Are you—?"

"I said *not another word*," snarled the gentle, scholarly woman who had been her dearest comfort for years. As the dancing lights swarmed around Caroline's tree, close enough to reveal the tiny, winged figures within them, the larger ball of light swept overhead. Juliana stepped into view, lit by its glow—and the expression on her lovely face looked astonishingly unfamiliar.

Caroline had never seen her in such a rage before. Fury flushed Juliana's fine features and sparked from her blue eyes like a lightning storm. It was shockingly, *outrageously* inappropriate to find that sight so viscerally attractive—but Juliana looked like a furious queen with that vivid blue gown swirling enticingly around her slim body and her magical power blazing for all to see. Caroline wanted to lunge forward and *devour*...or simply fall to her knees in awe.

She had given up her right to do either of those

things, though. So she only closed her lips as instructed and tilted her head questioningly at the dancing lights that circled them, stuffing down every inconvenient emotion that threatened to overcome all of her principles.

Juliana turned to the dancing lights, too, her chin still raised at an imperious angle. "Well?" she demanded. "Who do I have to bargain with to free her, then?"

Wait.

"What do you mean, *free* me?" Caroline demanded. "I came here to free you!"

"*What*?" Juliana swung back to stare at her...and a familiar figure stepped out from within Caroline's tree, separating from the bark with a soft *snick*.

"Oh, good." The guardian of the woods smiled with feline satisfaction, fresh leaves cascading from her shoulders. The tiny winged figures in their swirl of silver lights swept through the air to cluster in her twig-filled hair, nuzzling against her face with soft, wordless murmurs of affection. "You did both come after all," she said calmly. "I rather thought you might."

CAROLINE STARED at the fey woman, sickening realization spinning through her body and leaving her nauseous. "You told me Juliana had left the path."

"Oh, did I?" The guardian's thin lips curved wider, revealing a hint of wickedly sharp teeth. "Think carefully on the words I spoke, child. Did I *really* tell you exactly that?"

"They tricked us both." Juliana shook her head at Caroline with a sigh. "How could you have been so foolish?"

"*I*?" Caroline's jaw fell open at the unexpected jab. She snapped it shut again and drew herself up, seizing the advantage of her superior height. "I'm not the only one who fell for their ruse tonight, was I?"

"But *I* had good reason to come." Juliana scowled. "What was your excuse?"

"What do you mean, 'excuse'?'"

"*Enough.*" The sudden chill in the fey guardian's voice cast goosebumps skittering across Caroline's bare arms. "A better question for you two children to ask now might be: 'How may we safely return to Thornfell...ever?'"

Ahhh. Dread skittered down the back of Caroline's neck.

"I am a student of Miss Harwood's." Juliana's voice was bright and bell-like, a safe anchor to hold onto even as Caroline reeled inwardly. "I *know* the college of Thornfell has an official bargain with you and these woods. There can be no question of breaking that peace now—"

"Which is why," murmured the guardian, "we would have left you unharmed had you only chosen to stay on the path, *as agreed.*" The sharp tips of her teeth gleamed in the flickering silver light cast by her small companions as they whirled eagerly around her head, giggling with unnerving glee. "*That* was the bargain we negotiated and the bargain we maintain. If Miss Harwood didn't bother to teach her students that simple lesson, then only she can be to blame."

Juliana flinched visibly—but Caroline stepped forward to stand side-by-side with her former fiancée. "We would be happy to negotiate a bargain of our own," she said firmly. "My lady, *surely* it would do you far more good to have strong, active allies outside these woods than a single pair of useless prisoners within them."

"Ah, but the two of you aren't quite useless, are you? A magician and a politician, held within my own domain…" Leaves and twigs rustled within her hair as she shook her head in slow consideration. "There are so many worlds beyond your single mortal realm…and *so* many rulers who would hunger for such delicious playthings to enjoy. Why do you think I chose to lure you both here?"

Caroline's bare arm brushed against Juliana's slim, silk-covered shoulder. She didn't even know which of them had taken the first step closer…but she felt stronger when she stood next to Juliana. She always had.

Now, the warmth that radiated between them gave her the fire she needed to hold the guardian's inhuman green gaze and keep her own expression still and unimpressed. "We can offer you a better bargain than any of those rulers. You don't care nearly as much for any of their worlds. *These* woods have been your home for centuries. They're where you walked with your love when he still lived."

Gold flashed like lightning in the guardian's eyes. "That was a very long time ago."

"Only by mortal standards." Caroline had seen the look on the fey woman's face that last, terrible night in the woods, when she had glimpsed the pile of treasures that the Harwoods had brought as offerings: her lover's own private journals, stored for well over a century in some dusty Harwood attic, but still full of passionate, coded references to his beloved—her. It was the proof she had needed of his true devotion—and it had meant so much to her, it had transformed her from a bitter enemy of the Harwoods into their most dangerous protector.

...Which meant that none of her words now made sense—and there had to be a deeper, hidden intention behind all of the guardian's actions this evening.

Think like the politician you are! That mental order came in her aunt's voice, sharp and clear from thousands of real-life repetitions—and Caroline snapped to attention, her mind clicking through the familiar cycle of facts, dangers, and solutions. "Old agreements or not, you *know* you'll lose all cordial relations with the Harwoods if you start tricking their students and visitors off the paths. Why not maintain your new friendship with your neighbors *and* gain something else that you desire?"

The guardian's eyes narrowed. "And what is it that *you* imagine I could possibly desire, mortal child?"

Her voice dripped with disdain—but Caroline had been proving herself every day since she'd first been dropped off as a child in her famous aunt's grand country house, surrounded by intimidating, unfamiliar adults and seemingly impossible expectations at every turn.

She had met those expectations every time. Now she looked their deadly, magical captor in the eyes, called on every recollection of vulnerability she had ever glimpsed or inferred from the fey woman's actions, and said with all the confidence she had earned, "You want companionship, of course. You are terribly lonely. And you still miss your Harwood lover every day."

The guardian let out a feral hiss. "You understand *nothing* of true love!" She paced forward like a stalking animal, her predatory gaze fixed on Caroline's face. "I've *seen* your choices. If you imagine—"

"Oh, I might actually be able to help you with that!" The words flooded out of Juliana in a breathless rush. Her shoulders relaxed, and she grinned at the fey woman with sudden delight, as dazzling as a candle in the darkness. "I've recalled the right spell. If I can only see some of his old journals—well, of course it won't *really* be him even if it does work. No one can actually raise the dead! But if you wanted a memory of him to keep here, as vivid and true as I could make it…"

The guardian froze in midstep. Even the tiny silver fey around her head stilled in sudden, watchful—or frightened?—silence.

Facts, dangers, solutions. Every muscle in Caroline's body clenched tight in preparation.

She'd push Juliana out of the way with one arm and throw herself between them if the guardian took this as an insult and attacked. Then—

"That is not something human magic can achieve." The fey woman held herself still and taut, like an arrow waiting to be loosed.

Caroline shifted ever-so-slightly forward, just in case.

"Oh, it's a very old, obscure spell. No one I know has used it." Juliana didn't even seem to notice her own danger. "One of the Harwoods wrote it two centuries ago. I don't think he ever shared it with the world at large—it was for his own personal use, at most—but I found it tucked into the back of one of the old hand-written spellbooks in the school library last month. It was written in rather an archaic fashion, of course, but I analyzed it as an exercise, and the theory itself is completely sound."

Juliana always lost her shyness once a conversation turned to magic. Then, she positively *glowed.* Caroline could have listened to her for hours, without needing to understand a single technical detail along the way.

But there was no time to glory in her brilliance tonight, nor any chance of seducing all that shining intensity into incoherent delight afterwards. All that Caroline could hope for now was to keep her former fiancée alive for the rest of the evening—and Juliana, perfect though she was, wouldn't even notice an enraged rhinoceros charging towards her once she was absorbed in an interesting spell.

So Caroline spoke before Juliana could continue, her own gaze fixed firmly on their captor's face. "*That* is the bargain that we offer. She'll cast the spell, and you will let us go immediately afterwards."

"You foolish, foolish children." The fey guardian's face was a study in hunger…and lurking fury. "She may have studied it in theory, but what will you do when you find that she's mistaken? You can hardly win everything in that case, can you? Not without solving at least one riddle."

Facts, dangers, solutions. "You can keep me as a consolation prize if it doesn't work—but you'll still have to let Juliana go."

"Agreed," said the guardian—

And Juliana gave a sudden start, as if their words had only just filtered through her concentration. "Wait, what? *No!* You can't—"

"The bargain has been struck," said the fey woman with satisfaction. "You have until dawn."

She stepped into the tree, and its bark *snicked* closed around her. Her tiny silver followers shot away through the air, disappearing into the rustling trees beyond.

The mossy, root-tangled soil before Juliana's feet split open to disgorge a pile of ancient, leather-bound journals stacked on a blanket stitched of green leaves and golden glitter…

And Caroline and Juliana were left alone in the

darkness for the first time since their betrothal had ended.

* * *

As branches rustled tauntingly around her, Juliana's ribs became a burning cage, pressing inexorably inwards to squeeze her lungs shut.

What if she couldn't—

But if she couldn't—!

"There's no rush," Caroline said cheerfully. "We have until dawn, after all, so you should take all the time you need to prepare yourself. I know you won't need that long for the spell."

"How could you be so foolish?" Fury burst open the bars of her cage, and Juliana yanked her head up to glare at her erstwhile fiancée. "What were you *thinking*, promising your life away to her so recklessly? You can't—"

"I just did, actually." That unshakably stubborn tilt of Caroline's jaw had been familiar for years, but it had never before felt *so* infuriating. "We could spend this evening arguing over tiny details if that's what you choose, *or* instead, you could simply appreciate the fact that—"

"Appreciate?" Juliana stared at her in disbelief. "I stepped off the path tonight to *rescue* you. Why would I appreciate you throwing your life away now?"

"I was *trying* to protect you. Which I did!" Caroline glared directly back at her, breathing hard—which made her glorious bosom rise and fall exactly at the level of Juliana's eyes, cupped with loving closeness by her rich pink bodice.

Argh! Juliana forced her gaze away. She didn't have the right to ogle Caroline's bosom anymore. That privilege had been withdrawn scarcely an hour ago.

They were *supposed* to have spent this evening enjoying a glorious reunion. She wasn't supposed to be standing in the middle of the woods right now shrieking at her lost love like an emotional, irrational gentleman on a tirade. *None* of this was supposed to have happened at all…

But yet again, she hadn't been enough to prevent any of it.

"You don't have to mask your true feelings anymore." She dropped heavily down to her knees and lowered her head to investigate the pile of stacked journals. "I promise we don't need to argue more tonight."

What was the point? None of the furious reproaches that she'd been planning to spill over her jilting would do either of them any good at this point. Caroline was clearly already wracked with guilt. Why else would she have bargained away her own life to keep Juliana safe?

Juliana had never received such a poisonous gift.

Her spellcast ball of light hovered just above them, leaving her face safely shadowed as she let out a long sigh. "I just…can't bear to hear you say that you did this to protect me."

Silence hung over them for a long moment, broken only by the whisper of a breeze through the nearby branches.

The journal at the top of the pile was full of cramped, antique handwriting in a faded copper ink. It took real concentration to piece out the words in the top page.

I walked with my beloved in the woods today, spinning dreams that glittered like spidersilk in sunshine...

"Juliana..." Caroline's voice sounded wary. *As it should.* "Why else do you think I would have done it?"

"I'm not so helpless as you apparently think." Juliana refused to look up from the page. She *would not* let Caroline see tears sparkling in her eyes. Not now. "You didn't have to give yourself up for me just now, any more than you had to come running here to save me in the first place. I would have been *fine* without you."

"I know." Caroline's voice tightened. "I'm the reason you put yourself in danger tonight, in the first place."

"And I'm the reason *you* did." Juliana jerked her shoulders in a shrug, her vision blurring as she stared fiercely at the page. "The fey fooled us both. They are famously good at that." She shook her head, pressing her lips together for as long as she could...before the question finally burst out. "But *why* did you let yourself be fooled in the first place? Did you really think I was so pathetic—so *useless*—that I would have gone running off the paths tonight only because you'd jilted me?"

Breath sucked in through Caroline's teeth, above her head. "So...you're saying you weren't affected at all by the end of our betrothal? Or do you mean you were actually relieved, and *that* was why you agreed so quickly? If you changed your mind about me when you came to Thornfell and finally met other women who shared your own interests—"

"*What*?" Juliana almost dropped the journal. She gaped up at Caroline. "You imagine I've been...what? Having an *affair*? With one of my classmates?"

"Of course not." The words gritted out from Caroline's clenched jaw as she gazed fiercely out into the woods, only too obviously avoiding Juliana's eyes. "I know you would never betray a commitment once you'd made it. But I saw for myself, last spring, just how happy you were to be here among all the other women studying magic. If you've been secretly wishing to be released from our betrothal, you should have told me. I would have understood."

"Of course you would!" Juliana snorted out a humorless laugh as she looked back down at the journal in her hands. "Then you wouldn't have had to feel guilty about ending it yourself."

"You think I *wanted* to end it?" Caroline said hotly. "If I'd had any other choice—!"

"You had a choice, and you made it tonight...as was perfectly within your rights." Exhaustion swept through Juliana with the truth of her own words. What *was* the point of arguing anymore?

She knew exactly what it felt like to be with people

who didn't love her. She wouldn't fight to win that anymore.

Just end this and be done. "That's what I am trying to explain," she said softly. "I *know* you felt guilty about choosing your own career over your promises to me. You're too principled *not* to be distressed by that. But you didn't have to let guilt overcome your common sense. I am perfectly capable of taking care of myself. My well-being is no longer any of your concern—and I would never, *ever* give up your life for my safety."

There. She had said all that she'd had left to say.

This time, when she looked back down at the page, her vision didn't blur by so much as a fraction. She could make out the words perfectly well.

All she had to do now was find a way to make one old spell work. Then she could bury herself safely in books for the rest of her life, and she would never have to engage in another heart-shattering conversation like this one again.

The spell itself, of course, was predicated on the absorption of a significant amount of writing from its subject. If she'd had all the time in the world, she could have simply read those words herself. With only a limited number of hours available, though, the question of how to most effectively absorb them would be—

"*Juliana!*" Her name came from surprisingly nearby, and with an unmistakable edge of frustration; blinking, she realized that Caroline had dropped down to kneel beside her at some point.

There *had* been a vague hum of background noise, now that Juliana thought of it. Could Caroline have said her name more than once?

"I beg your pardon," she said, her gaze already sliding back to the page, "but—"

"This *matters,*" said Caroline, and set one strong hand over the lines of faded text, blocking them from view. "Do you actually believe that I chose my career over *you* tonight?"

Juliana's mind went still. She drew a steadying breath, keeping her eyes fixed safely on that hand and away from Caroline's too-penetrating gaze. "You needn't suffer any guilt on that account. I know I lost my temper unjustly, but the truth is, I have always understood your priorities. I won't berate you any longer."

"But I don't think you do understand," said Caroline, "because for the last three years, Juliana, *you* have been my highest priority. *Always,*" she added firmly, as Juliana's head jerked up and their gazes finally met.

Juliana gaped at her in utter disbelief. "Why would you say this to me now? I've already released you from our betrothal. I *told* you—"

"But you released me for your sake, not for mine." Caroline gave a half-laugh as she shook her head, fingers curling with tension above the page where they lay. "If I'm going to sacrifice what I most want in the world—"

"Everyone in Angland knows what you most want in the world," said Juliana. "A place in the Boudiccate.

That's why we've had to stay a secret all of these years —because nothing could ever be allowed to threaten that goal. Certainly not me."

She wasn't proud of the bitterness that laced her voice...but she wasn't as shocked by it as Caroline seemed to be.

Her ex-fiancée stumbled backwards, nearly falling. Her hand dropped away from Juliana's book as she said, "Is that—have you actually—*all this time*—"

"If you'll forgive me," said Juliana, "I have a spell to work and a limited amount of time to manage it. So, if you could simply accept that I've *always* known the truth and you needn't hide it behind diplomatic phrases any longer..." She dipped her head back down to stare fiercely at the book in her hands, before she could forget everything she'd told herself about pride and justice and start casting *real* magic all over the place.

CAROLINE'S HEAD was buzzing as if a hive of bees had taken nest within it—and the sight of Juliana coolly retreating into that damned book to erect an invisible barrier between them was unbearable.

She shoved herself inelegantly to her feet. "You *swore* to me that you understood why we had to keep it a secret!" she snarled. "We agreed on that *together*, all those years ago. I *never*—"

"What more do you want of me, Caroline?" The

book fell to the ground as the ball of light above it burst suddenly upwards through the air, blazing with hot, tightly contained flames. Juliana rose with it, kicking her enveloping blue skirts out of her way, her gaze blindingly heated. "For three years, I have agreed to *every single thing* you ever asked from me!"

She counted off the points on one small hand, her voice rising to a near-bellow. "First, I pretended not to have any claim on you in public. Then last year, when matters became more dangerous, I let you start looking past me as if you didn't even know me. Tonight, I let you step away from *every* promise you'd ever made to me, without a single word of protest. And now...now, you're waiting for me to say *what*? That I never minded in the first place? Or that you've somehow done the right thing?"

She shook her head violently, her blonde hair falling out of its elaborate updo to curve wildly around her face. "It's too much, Caroline. This time, you're finally asking too much from me. I've spent all my life fighting to please the people who were meant to love me, and *I can't do it anymore.* I have friends and colleagues now, and they've taught me to value myself higher than that."

She was a goddess made of flame, blazing with light and heat.

She was everything Caroline had ever dreamed of...and she was *unimaginably* deluded.

"You have *never* had to agree with me in order to please me," Caroline said. "You've never had to prove anything to me. I'm the one who's not good enough for *you* anymore. How can that not be blindingly obvious?"

Juliana flung out her arms. "If you can't even take me seriously enough to be honest now…"

It only took one quick stride forward to seize those delicate, familiar hands in hers. "*Listen to me*, Julie. I'm begging you!" Caroline shook her head as she gazed down into those ferociously beautiful blue eyes. "I don't know what I did wrong all those years ago, to make you think I didn't care. I thought you agreed with all of our plans for the future, every time we discussed them. I'm so sorry I was wrong. I swear I would have listened if you'd ever uttered a word of disagreement—and tonight…" She swallowed hard. "I would have given *anything* for you to refuse to let me go."

Juliana's fair eyebrows crinkled. "But you *said*—"

"I made you a promise," Caroline said doggedly, "and despite what everyone in Angland thinks of me nowadays, my word can be trusted."

"But—"

"I swore to you three years ago that if you only had patience and faith in me, I *would* reach the Boudiccate, just as everyone said, and the two of us would rise together. *That's* what you deserve. It was the one thing I could offer you that no other woman could—not even your fellow students or—"

"Caro, *stop*!" Juliana yanked her hands free, staring at Caroline as if she'd suddenly started raving rather than simply laying out the truth between them. "What did I ever do to make you think me so mercenary?"

Caroline blinked, baffled. "What's mercenary about it? It's what *everyone* expected, not just you. I've known what I was meant to do ever since I was eight years old —no, wait, before that, when Aunt Honoria first told my parents that she'd chosen me as her heir, so they shifted me away from the other children. *Everyone* was counting on it. You know that! You told me you'd heard those rumors well before we ever met."

"Only because my aunt wouldn't stop hammering politics into my ears, in hopes that I'd finally start taking an interest. Caroline..." Juliana didn't look furious anymore. Her brow had furrowed into that characteristic look of concentration she wore when she was attempting a particularly tricky spell. This time, all that analytical focus had been turned on Caroline herself. Caroline's skin burned with the heat of it. "Why did you come alone to this party?"

"Who would have come with me?" Caroline asked wearily. "A whole cohort of friends always wanted to be seen with the famous Miss Fennell, but when it comes to the *disgraced* Miss Fennell..."

Juliana frowned harder. "What did your parents think of your aunt's sudden retirement?"

Caroline gave a jerky shake of her head, holding hard to the cool, hard shield that she'd built against that very question over the past months. "What else *could* they think of it? Either I must have been involved in Aunt Honoria's wrongdoings, or—since no one outside these grounds has evidence of any such wrong-doings—perhaps Aunt Honoria *actually* retired early, without waiting for me to take on her mantle, because she'd been disappointed in my efforts so far."

That had been Caroline's mother's own theory, only thinly disguised behind the bitterly careful phrasings in her final letter.

Caroline had burned that letter to ashes. Still, every word of it was imprinted in her memory.

"They expressed disappointment on my behalf, of course," she continued with practiced calm, "but, naturally, we all understood that they couldn't risk being associated with me anymore—not with my younger sisters still so uncertain of their own futures, *and* both hoping to earn themselves roles in our local city offices."

"So they're punishing *you* for what she did?" Juliana's voice spiraled. "And your aunt didn't have anything to say about that?"

Caroline's lips tightened against her will. After a moment she replied, as lightly as possible, "No one knows what my aunt has to say about anything, anymore. Apparently, she's endured more than enough company for a lifetime."

Juliana's eyes widened. She opened her mouth as if to speak—and then closed it again.

Caroline could only be grateful for that.

"At any rate," she said, "I'm under no illusions. I'm lucky to still have a post at all—and I've only managed to keep it this long because it's located so far out, in the upper edge of beyond, away from all society. If I'm *very* lucky and I work hard for years, keeping my head down and well away from controversy, then at some point I might even be able to advance a bit. But the idea of soaring to the Boudiccate in ten more years, the way I promised you—"

"Caroline," said Juliana, "tell me something. Whom do you plan to marry?"

Jolted, Caroline stared at her. "What are you talking about?"

Juliana crossed her arms. "It's a very simple question. What are your current plans for marriage?"

Caroline's laugh came out with a jagged edge. "I thought we'd agreed on *that* earlier this evening. I have no plans for marriage anymore."

"So you're not planning to wed a suitable gentleman mage once the rumors pass? To give yourself that extra chance at the Boudiccate?"

Caroline's spine stiffened.

It wasn't an unreasonable question. It was what Aunt Honoria herself had done. Caroline had planned to take that expected step in her own turn, too...until the night she'd met Juliana three years ago, when everything had changed.

Now, the very idea of choosing such a bloodless marital compromise, after spending three *years* joyfully anticipating a lifelong union of souls and bodies with the most dazzling woman she had ever met...

She flinched. "*Never.*"

"Why not?" Juliana looked at her steadily in their quiet circle of light.

There was no space for half-truths or self-protection in that small circle surrounded by darkness. Caroline had nothing left but brutal honesty now. After everything else she had revealed about herself—disgraced, humiliated, and yet still yearning for what she knew she no longer deserved—what was the point in hiding anymore? "No one else in the world could possibly replace you," she said flatly. "It would be a sacrilege."

"*Oh!*"

This time, it was Juliana who lunged forward—and Caroline was too shocked to even think of resisting when the love of her life landed against her with that exquisite combination of thrill and comfort that she had never expected to experience again.

Slim arms wrapped around her neck. Soft curves pressed against hers, making Caroline gasp with that gorgeously familiar, sharp, lancing *need*...

And then Juliana's lips finally, *finally* pressed against hers.

Caroline had stepped into the Harwoods' enchanted woods that evening with the firm intention of being ruled by hard common sense and steely principles. She had sworn that she would stand fast against all temptations to resist the path that she knew she needed to take.

But they had both stepped off the path tonight, and there was no going back. She pressed Juliana even closer in a breathless kiss that was wholly unrestrained, heedless of all possible reservations...

And the magic that shot through her veins as they kissed had nothing to do with the spellcasting that was taught in the school nearby.

Juliana's clever fingers worked their way against her scalp, tugging her closer still. *One breath, one soul...*

It was a fragment of poetry that Caroline thought she had forgotten ages ago. She had never had time to spend reading poetry when she had a dazzling career to build.

But Juliana's waist was poetry itself, warm and soft and welcoming beneath the silk that stroked against Caroline's searching fingers. She could have studied it for hours. And that delicious curve that sloped up from Juliana's waist to her bosom...

Juliana pulled her head back just far enough to yank a deep breath of air, her pupils dilated so intensely that they nearly swallowed up all the blue from her eyes. "Caroline," she gasped, "you utter *fool*." Laughter trembled in her voice as she shook her head. "How could you possibly think I only cared for your career?"

"How could *you* think I didn't adore you?" Caroline pressed herself even tighter against her love, until they could never be peeled apart by anyone ever again. "You are the *only* goal I ever chose for myself in all my life. Didn't you even notice? I would give up anything else to please you."

"You don't have to give up anything," Juliana said,

"*especially* not me. Never again! How could you be so cruel?"

"How could you ever think that I *wanted* to?" Caroline began...and then stopped. *Think like the politician you are.* She had all of the clues; she'd only been too blinded by her own fog of confusion and pain to see them. "Your aunt and father are both idiots," she said harshly. "The fact that they couldn't see for themselves what an amazement you are—"

"Let's not start discussing each other's families now," said Juliana. "If I start on what I think of some of *your* family's decisions—!"

"Not tonight," Caroline agreed, and buried her face in Juliana's soft blonde hair. "Oh, God." Shivers swept in a sudden, overwhelming wave through her body, and her grip turned desperate. "*Oh, my God.* I almost lost you! We would never have held each other like this again."

"We can't ever lose each other again." Juliana growled the words into Caroline's throat with fierce intensity, slim arms firm around Caroline's shoulders and warm breath sending thrills up and down Caroline's bare neck. "No more misunderstandings or noble sacrifices from either of us. I mean it! If you *ever* dare try to put me aside for my own good *ever again*, Caroline Fennell, I will cast a spell to bind you to my side forever, just so I can spend the rest of our lives telling you *exactly* what I think of that nonsense!"

"I will fall to my knees in gratitude," Caroline said fervently. "I'll do that now, if you'd like."

"Well, if you'd really *like* to go to your knees—no, wait." The deliciously teasing lilt to Juliana's voice disappeared. "Caroline!" Gasping, she thrust herself backwards, and Caroline released her with intense reluctance. "I can't believe we both forgot!"

Juliana groaned as she darted a quick glance at the starry sky through the canopy of leaves. "I still have a spell to perform before we can go free, and I haven't even worked out how to absorb all of these books in time."

"You will." Warmth filled Caroline like bright sunshine on a cloudless day as she gazed through the shadows at her delightfully disheveled fiancée, whose spellcast ball of light was bouncing through the air a full three feet away, apparently forgotten. "I've *never* had any doubts about your brilliance."

"Well, that's lovely, but—*argh*!" Juliana pulled even more hair free of her updo as she tugged at it with both hands. "I can't even think anymore. You've confounded me!"

"I have always enjoyed doing that." Caroline gave her a slow, deliberate smirk. "If it would help with inspiration—"

"No!" A gust of laughter escaped from Juliana's lips, but she pointed imperiously at the ground with one hand as she beckoned back her spellcast light with the other. "*Sit*," she ordered, "and don't distract me any longer! I have to solve this puzzle before dawn, and I can't do that while you're looking at me like that."

"Like what, precisely?" Caroline inquired. "Like I

want to devour you? Or—" She stopped, laughing and raising her hands in defense, as Juliana sent the ball of light whizzing straight at her head. "Very well! I surrender." Ducking beneath the fiery missile, she sat down on the blanket of leaves, tucking her skirts around her, and folded her hands primly together. "I won't even look in your direction," she promised. "I'll just sit very quietly and think to myself about..." Lips curving wickedly, she finished in a low, husky murmur: "*Distractions*."

"Shh!" Juliana sat down behind her with a thump, scooping up the top book from the pile and bending over it in pointed silence.

A moment later, though, Juliana scooted backwards, still reading, until their backs were firmly touching, warm and linked and certain—the way they had always been meant to be, together, ever since the very beginning.

That first night, three years ago, when Caroline had spotted Juliana in the shadows of a tedious political house party, their gazes had connected with stunning force—and her entire world had snapped into a new focus. Sudden clarity had sharpened every view as energy surged through her veins. She'd felt more tinglingly alive than ever before—and she still did whenever they were physically together.

No wonder she'd spent these last few months feeling as if she was drowning in a hopeless fog, with no steady ground left beneath her feet. She'd been keeping intentionally far from Juliana—and even before that, they'd spent months publicly distancing themselves from each other to protect Caroline's political ambitions.

It all seemed so foolish now...no, *more* than foolish, if Juliana had suffered real pain from that decision, no matter how calmly she'd agreed to it at the time. How had Caroline not realized that that was a façade? She'd have to push much harder in the future—make certain her fiancée knew that it was always safe to disagree with her, no matter what different rules had been imprinted in Juliana's childhood.

To build that full trust, though, would take real time and effort of the sort that wasn't easy at great distances.

They'd spent so long apart already...

"Aha!" Beaming, Juliana twisted around on the blanket of leaves and waved her book triumphantly. "I've thought up a way to absorb all of these at once, without my having to read through them myself."

"Excellent." The sooner the better, as far as Caroline was concerned. The more she thought about the dilemmas ahead, the more her skin prickled with the urgent need to sneak past all the glittering bustle of the outdoor ball, into the quiet old bricks of Thornfell itself and to a private room behind a door that locked, as quickly as possible. She needed to strip that borrowed gown off Juliana's body and prove to both of them—once and for all—that their reconciliation was real and tangible, not merely a wistful dream sparked by these fey woods.

She had to *know* it wouldn't shatter when they left the woods behind.

Juliana stood up, dusting off her hands, and stepping off the blanket. "Help me?"

"Always," Caroline said, and followed her example.

Together, they lifted the four corners of the blanket, holding the piled books cupped between them. At Juliana's direction, Caroline stepped forward to take the third and fourth corners, too, holding the full pile steady as Juliana lifted her arms above it and began to chant her spell.

Reddish-gold specks flickered into life above the books, like hot sparks cast off by a bonfire. As Caroline watched, they multiplied into a bright cloud that streamed upward through the night air, winding around and around Juliana's slim body until it encircled her chest and face and she was utterly surrounded by heatless flame.

Through its red glow, Caroline saw her mouth open wide into a sudden yell—

And even as she instinctively started forward, the cloud of sparks surged forward, shooting into her fiancée's mouth until it had been swallowed up entirely.

Red flames glowed behind the whites of Juliana's eyes. She let out a shuddering breath, her shoulders slumping.

"Well." Her voice was shadowed by a man's deeper one, ringing underneath her own in unsettling near-unison. "At least *that* spell worked properly."

* * *

IT HAD NEVER FELT so difficult for Juliana to think.

Even the wild anemones this year have only half-bloomed; perhaps they suffer the same forebodings my sisters habitually express over breakfast in this year of upheavals in the world beyond our borders...

Juliana couldn't have identified a wild anemone to save her life, and she certainly hadn't any sisters. But then, those weren't her words at all. It was an unfamiliar male voice that filled her head to overflowing with scholarly notes on natural history, detailed discourses on the different seasons in the woods, wistful hints at his secret and forbidden beloved, whom none of his family could be allowed to meet...

Not my beloved! Juliana remembered, and pulled herself free from the morass with a snap as her own ferociously *present* beloved yelled—possibly not for the first time: "*Juliana!*"

"I'm here!" Juliana clapped her hands to her ears, beset by noise within and without. "You needn't shout."

"But who's answering me now?" Caroline's eyes looked wild in the dim light. "I can hear someone else's voice when you speak!"

"Oh, can you?" Juliana brightened. That *was* a fascinating side-effect...

...but, clearly, a distressing one to her fiancée, who'd been through quite enough emotional turmoil already. Sighing, she decided not to explore that phenomenon any further tonight, intriguing though the implications might be. She would simply save that experimentation for later. "Don't worry," she said. "I only have to hold his words for a few more minutes while I sort out the final spell."

"Good." Caroline grimaced. "Do you recall how I said I don't *ever* want you to be anyone but yourself, without pretenses? I meant it. Get him out!"

Juliana gave a started half-laugh. "I never went *this* far before," she murmured.

It was true. She'd never actively pretended to be anyone else when she'd been with Caroline—not the way she'd had to pretend in her own family home for years, keeping her head safely lowered and her responses meek, with only the fire of her own secret resistance burning within her until she was old enough to claim her maternal inheritance and be free of her rigidly disapproving aunt's control.

She'd never *meant* to pretend anything with Caroline at all—so, until tonight, she'd hardly even realized that she had.

In theory, she really had agreed with every plan that they had made for their future. How could she not? Theoretically, it *should* have been perfectly acceptable to keep their betrothal a secret when it was suggested for such eminently sensible reasons. To someone who knew all of those reasons, it *should* have been uncontroversial for her secret fiancée to ignore her in public.

In fact, it had never even occurred to her that she

could protest, when Caroline's reasons made so much theoretical sense...

But as she had learned since beginning her studies at Thornfell, there was *always* a difference between theory and practice. She had proven herself by now as a student of academic theory, but she was only just beginning to understand her own, irrational heart... and exactly how it had been affected by a lifetime of lessons from the people who should have cared for it most deeply.

She wouldn't be so careless now with Caroline's distress, no matter how irrational that distress might seem to her. So she focused all of her Thornfell-honed brain, through the endless waves of notes and discourses and hopeless longings from a mind not her own, on that single, two-hundred-year-old spell that she had uncovered and analyzed in the Harwoods' library.

All she had to do was focus her intention and the angles of the spell exactly right, speak the right words in the proper intonation, and then...!

Light overwhelmed her.

She fell to her knees...

And through the blinding golden light that suddenly blazed through the woods, a figure formed between her and her fiancée.

A man bent over his desk, writing busily with an antique quill pen. Light streamed through his lean body. His voice murmured through the air, an elegant, abstracted tenor reading out loud as he wrote.

"When the cowslips first fade, the end of spring..."

Juliana's jaw dropped open as his words streamed on outside the confines of her head—which was solely her own once again.

She met her fiancée's wide eyes through his translucent figure as Caroline shifted forward, her mouth falling open with a deeply satisfying look of wonder. Juliana *had* been right about that untested, forgotten old spell. The theory behind it truly did work!

But as one of the ash trees before her opened with a soft *snick!* and the guardian of the woods stepped out to join them, she had the sudden and horribly queasy feeling that once again, theory and practice might not have quite matched up after all.

* * *

CAROLINE COULD NEVER HAVE MISTAKEN the gentleman before her as anyone but a Harwood.

It wasn't merely that steady blue gaze, so like the modern Jonathan Harwood's; it was the intensity with which he approached his self-imposed task—that clear and unshakeable conviction on his part that whatever he was currently attempting *was* the most important goal in the entire world, and he would either conquer it or else die trying—with his family wholeheartedly on his side regardless of what anyone else thought of him.

Whether one admired the Harwoods—as Caroline

did, with a wistful tinge of envy for that unbreakable family unity—or hated them, as many of their rivals across the nation did, there *was* a reason that they had been a family of eccentric power for centuries on end.

Even when she stepped close enough that she could have touched his translucent arm if she'd dared, he still didn't look up from his self-appointed task.

She cleared her throat politely. "Ahem—"

An unmistakable soft *snick!* sounded behind her.

A harshly indrawn breath followed it.

Caroline whirled around, goosebumps popping up all along her spine. "It isn't dawn yet!"

"But she's cast the spell—and I found that I couldn't wait to see it after all."

The guardian's gaze was fixed on that bent, busy figure with a hunger so raw, it should never have been witnessed by anyone outside their partnership. Her whole body formed an arc of yearning, like a silver birch tree curving in the wind.

How desperate would *Caroline* feel if she'd lost Juliana for more than an hour—if they had been parted for *centuries* instead? It was unthinkable. *Unbearable.*

But instead of taking pride in her work, Juliana threw out a hand in warning, her tone full of anguish. "Wait!"

Of course she didn't wait. Caroline couldn't have managed it, either.

Ignoring Juliana, the guardian flowed forward, long, trembling, branch-like fingers outstretched—

And she passed directly through the translucent form of her lost beloved, stumbling and nearly falling to the ground. It was the first time Caroline had ever glimpsed such lack of grace in any fey, and the sight sent a stab of primal fear through her chest.

Danger...

She was moving before she could even think, hurrying to place herself between Juliana and the guardian...

Whose own great love didn't even look up from his work as his voice murmured gently on and on. "The leaves are already beginning to shift color by the brook. The rest of the woods cannot lag far behind..."

"She told you it wouldn't really be him!" Caroline's voice was too loud, too urgent. It was the wrong approach for negotiation, and she knew it. She couldn't help herself, though. That unguarded anguish in the fey woman's eyes spoke directly to the wounded part of her own heart—that secret corner that hadn't quite recovered yet from losing her own love that night, even if her loss had only lasted for an hour.

How much worse would it be to be presented with an uncaring, uninterested and untouchable vision of Juliana, dangled before her like a false promise—or, even worse, a taunt?

It was a mistake," Juliana said miserably behind her. "Forgive me. Please. I was only thinking of the theory behind the spell, not...not how it would actually feel, when it was done."

"She still completed her part of the bargain,

though," said Caroline. Taking a deep breath, she dropped to one knee on the mossy ground and bent her head with all the grace that she'd been taught in years of diplomatic lessons. "My lady, your terms for her have been fulfilled. According to your bargain, she must now be allowed to leave."

"What? Wait a minute!" Juliana started forward, grabbing Caroline's shoulder in a firm grip. "What do you mean, *I* must be allowed? I'm not leaving you alone here!"

Alone was the look in the fey woman's eyes as she stared, heedless of any of their words, at the translucent man before them, so indifferent to her gaze. *Alone* was what Caroline had so carelessly diagnosed in her, such a short time ago.

The spell itself might have worked, but how could she ever have imagined that a *memory* of the guardian's love would ever be enough to give her the company she craved? Even when Caroline and Juliana had written letters—passionate, detailed letters—to each other three times a week, they'd still ended up with a gradual accumulation of misunderstandings that had built, across the years, into a morass that nearly led to their ruin. *Nothing* could ever replace true physical companionship—that day-to-day sharing of life with all its tribulations and adventures.

...The kind that she had never granted Juliana or herself because she'd always been so driven to achieve her family's goals, regardless of her own personal happiness.

So much wasted time...

Even as she thought those words, the guardian's gaze shifted, at last, to meet hers. Pain drew tight lines around the fey woman's mouth, but her voice was steady and her hazel eyes were clear once more as she looked up at Caroline. "Well? What of your part in all of this? I did warn you that the spell wouldn't be enough—but even I couldn't resist this glimpse when it was offered, and you had to see it for yourself to understand." Her sigh sent leaves rippling on trees all around the clearing.

"My...part?" Caroline blinked, snapping back into focus as her attention snagged on the layered nuances in the fey woman's voice.

She *had* offered herself as a hostage for the success of Juliana's spell when she'd first negotiated their bargain—but the guardian's words seemed to carry more weight than that.

Rapidly, she ran back through the details of their full negotiation. She'd spent years practicing that skill with her aunt, being tested until she could repeat any careless line that she'd overheard from anyone, no matter how insignificant it had seemed at the time.

So...she had offered up their bargain—*"She'll cast the spell, and you will let us go immediately afterwards."*

But the guardian hadn't immediately accepted it. What had she said, exactly, when she'd questioned whether Juliana's spell would even work?

"What if she's mistaken? You can hardly win every-

thing in that case, can you? Not without solving at least one riddle."

A riddle. *Of course!* It was the oldest fey bargaining chip in known history. But was she expected to ask for one now, or....?

Oh.

Caroline's gaze took in the tableau of pain before her—of loss, of connections missed forevermore—and her mouth dropped open.

The riddle was obvious, wasn't it? It had even been spoken out loud by the guardian, the challenge dropped so lightly into conversation.

"Why do you think I chose to lure you both here?"

Why would the guardian of these woods risk her newfound peace and friendship with the Harwood family only to steal two women from their party, so soon after swearing her protection to Thornfell? And why had she chosen Caroline and Juliana, in particular?

"I know the answer to your riddle," Caroline breathed.

The backs of her eyes burned; she dashed a quick hand across them, fighting for breath as she took in the magnitude of what had been done.

It was never polite to say *thank you* to any fey. But:

"I will cherish your gift all my life," she murmured, and she bent her head sincerely.

"Caroline?" Juliana's voice was still strung tight with fear above her. "What are you talking about? *What* riddle? What—?"

"I'll leave you two to discuss that at your leisure." The guardian's voice crackled with weariness, like autumn leaves. "You'll do it outside, though, if you please. I require a moment of privacy with my old memories now."

Vines shot up beneath Caroline's legs and Juliana's feet and grasped both of them before they could resist. A moment later, they were hurtling inexorably through the trees, whose branches pushed them faster and faster along their way…

Until, finally, they stood together, panting, on the safety of the human path, clutching at each other's scratched arms to keep upright.

"What—*what*?" Juliana demanded. "What just happened? Why did she let you go after all?"

"She didn't want to keep us in the first place," Caroline said breathlessly. "That was *never* her true purpose. She is still the guardian of these woods and a friend to Thornfell's students, after all. She witnessed everything between us earlier—and she gave us a gift beyond compare."

"But… *Oh!*" Juliana's eyes widened. "You mean—?"

"She heard us jilt each other," Caroline said, "and she *knew* we were being fools. You saw how she looked at the vision of her Harwood—she'd give anything to win any more moments with him. So she chose *not* to stand back tonight and allow us to throw away all the time that we could still have together."

"*Oh.*" Juliana's eyes shone; she sniffed, inelegantly,

as tears traced their ways down her cheeks. "We can't leave her alone forever, either."

"We won't," Caroline said. "She'll have my friendship and my gratitude as long as I live, and we'll find a way to make tonight up to her, somehow. I swear it. But Juliana..." She grasped her fiancée's right hand and raised it to her lips, fighting against her own tears—of relief, of gratitude, and of sheer, quaking terror of what she had so nearly missed. "Thank you for stepping off the path to find me tonight. *Thank you*."

Juliana's free hand curved around her cheek. "*And you.*" She tipped her head forward until it rested against the hollow of Caroline's neck, where it fit perfectly. "We'll always be there for each other, from now on."

"We will," Caroline vowed, "and close at hand, too. I'm never making any plans by letter ever again. I need to actually see your face whenever we're making our decisions."

"I beg your pardon?" Blinking, Juliana lifted her head. "I still have at least three more years left at Thornfell, and you're stationed at the upper end of beyond—"

"Which is why I'll be giving up my position." A rush of exhilaration flooded through Caroline at the astonishing liberation of her own reckless words.

She didn't have to force herself to put aside her own needs any longer. Her family had already given her up when they'd surrendered their hopes of her reaching the Boudiccate. Perhaps Honoria, at least, would one day resurface and see past her own shame to welcome Caroline back—but regardless, Caroline had lost the golden anchor that had tied her down for years. Who cared what was sensible or practical anymore?

"I'm going to be brave," she said on that gust of liberation, "and ask Amy Harwood if she has any need for an assistant to work here at the Harwood estate. If she won't hire me because of my aunt, I'll understand —but then I'll find something else to do nearby. I can't bear to be so far from you ever again."

"If worst comes to worst, I'll buy you a cottage myself!" Juliana said giddily. "I'll sneak out after dark to have secret rendezvous with you every night."

"Or we could forget about keeping ourselves secret at all." Caroline's heart was hammering so intensely that she felt faint—but Juliana's hand was firm in hers, Juliana was nestled against her chest, and she was home at last, in the place where she belonged. "I know I'm not the famous Miss Fennell anymore," she said, "but I still want to meet your friends. I want everyone to know that you're mine and I'm yours. I—"

Juliana's lips closed over hers before she could finish her sentence, and Caroline melted into her kiss.

They would have plenty of time to talk over details later.

They had all the rest of their lives.

Juliana was walking arm in arm with Caroline half an hour later, her head tipped cozily against Caroline's left shoulder, when she spotted lights in the distance. She straightened. "Those aren't—?"

"They look like torches to me." Caroline straightened too, brushing down her gown. The grass stains might never be removable, but in the dim light that Juliana had cast, they just might not be noticed by any careless onlookers. "The ball can't have ended yet already, can it?"

"Not for hours, surely." Frowning, Juliana peered through the distance...

And smiled as the voices finally grew close enough to recognize.

"*There* you are!" Turning the corner of the path, her friends flew towards her in a mass of noisy, loving concern.

"We couldn't find you anywhere!"

"At first we thought you'd just run off from the crowds—"

"Someone said they'd seen fey lights in the woods—"

"We were worried—"

"We should have known you were just chatting to someone interesting in the quiet, but—"

"It wasn't any fun without you anyway," said Willa Koh, "so why *would* we choose to stay?"

As they all clustered around Juliana—with looks of wide-eyed interest at Caroline, who still stood close beside her—Miss Harwood and her husband stood back, watching quietly.

Mr. Wrexham gave Juliana a small, approving nod as he took in the neat ball of light that floated behind her.

Miss Harwood's lips twitched as she looked directly at the grass stains on Caroline's gown.

"Well," she said firmly, "it seems a rescue party wasn't required after all, so if everyone would like to return to the ball for our final magical demonstrations—"

"Wait." Surrounded by her friends—no, her *family* —and her love, Juliana stepped forward and reached out to openly clasp Caroline's hands in hers. "First, I want to introduce everyone to my new—and my old— fiancée."

Formal balls would always be a trial to a lady with more interest in ancient spells than modern fashion. But as she and Caroline were enveloped by delighted hugs and exclamations—and as fey eyes watched with approval from the rustling trees beyond—Juliana had to confess: tonight's ball truly had been worth all of the effort.

AFTERWORD

If you're one of my long-time readers, you'll already know that *Moontangled* is the latest novella in The Harwood Spellbook. If you're new to the series, though, you can go back to the beginning (and see Caroline and Juliana's first appearances!) in *Snowspelled*, which Ilona Andrews called 'clever, romantic and filled with magic.' (They also have important roles to play in *Snowspelled*'s direct sequel, *Thornbound*, and you can read Amy Harwood's own origin story in the prequel novella, *Spellswept*.)

I hope you'll enjoy the further adventures of the Harwoods and their friends!

If you've already read your way through the Harwood Spellbook and you'd like to read more frothy, fun stories from me, check out *The Wrong Foot* or *Courting Magic* (which is set in an entirely different alt-Regency world, following up on my earlier Regency fantasy series, *Kat, Incorrigible)*. I also have a YA f/f romantic fantasy novelette available, *The Disastrous Début of Agatha Tremain,* which is set in an entirely different version of Victorian England. (I love historical fantasy!)

I've also written two darker adult historical fantasy novels set in the real-life Habsburg empire, *Masks and Shadows* and *Congress of Secrets*, along with multiple MG fantasy adventure novels. My most recent trilogy began with *The Dragon with a Chocolate Heart*, which won the 2017 Cybils Award for Best Elementary/MG Speculative Fiction novel and was chosen as A Might Girl Book of the Year for 2017.

To stay up to date with all of my new releases (and get the chance to win advance reading copies of my new books, too!), sign up for my newsletter here:

www.stephanieburgis.com/newsletter

You can get early copies of my ebooks and read my monthly Dragons' Book Club column (where my readers trade fabulous recs of their own!) at my Patreon:

www.patreon.com/stephanieburgis

And if you have the time and energy to review *Moontangled* online, I would be incredibly grateful. Word-of-mouth makes such a difference.

Thanks for joining me in my writing adventures!

ACKNOWLEDGMENTS

Thank you so much to all of the readers who asked for a story about Miss Fennell and Miss Banks—thereby empowering me to write *exactly* what I'd most wanted to write next!—and who voted in my Facebook and Twitter polls to help me decide on the perfect title.

Thank you to Ravven for creating such a perfect cover for my story.

Thank you to Jenn Reese, Claire Fayers, Tiffany Trent and Amber Lough for really helpful feedback on the second draft. Thank you to Tiffany Trent for careful and generous copyediting, too.

Thank you to Gemma Beynon for wonderfully timed talks on art and motherhood and perfectionism —and for firmly instructing me *not* to beat myself up if I took a week longer to complete this novella than I had originally planned! I am very lucky in my friends.

Thank you to sharp-eyed readers Llinos Cathryn

Wynn-Jones, Roberta Reads, Julia Linthicum, and Jen Larsen for catching those last few sneaky typos just in time.

Thank you to Helen Kord at *All Booked Up* for a really good review note that helped me figure out an important change that I've now made to the first scene of this book.

Thank you to Patrick Samphire for additional beautiful cover design on the paperback edition, and for so much emotional and practical support throughout.

And a huge thanks to the Dragon Lords, Dragon Rulers, Dragon Angels and more on my Patreon page who've given me such a wonderful boost of support so that I can relax and have fun creating more and more stories to share with everybody. Joanna, Amanda Taylor-Chaisson, Amber Alexander, Brooke Johnson, D. Franklin and Zoe Johnson, Emily Lyman, Emma Rose Ribbons, Gabe Krabbe, Heather Holt, Jenni Nock, Julia Knowles, Julia Linthicum, Karen Kisner, Karen Riegle, Katharine, Katherine, Kathy Martin, Lab, Lindsay Eager, Lisa M. Richardson, Lisa Moore, Lydia San Andres, Marissa Lingen, Melita Kennedy, Nan Klock, Norma Guzman, Rachel Halpern, Robert Dean, S.P., Sara Carmody, Tahmi DeSchepper, The SF Reader, Vickie R., Edmond Hyland, Jacqueline Seamon, Jenn Reese, Katrina Middelburg, Konstanze Tants, Laura B., Llinos Cathryn Wynn-Jones, Medusa's Mirror, Navessa Allen, Sally, Solomon Foster, and

Vivian Behrman: *Thank you*. I appreciate you all so much, and your support makes such a difference to me!

Printed in Great Britain
by Amazon

79279584R00058